THE JOURNEY'S QUEST

ERNEST & CHRISTINE SOLAR
ILLUSTRATED BY MICHELLE WALKER

INDIE OWL PRESS KIDS

4700 Millenia Blvd
Ste 175 #90776
Orlando, FL 32839

info@indieowlpress.com
IndieOwlPress.com

THE JOURNEY'S QUEST

Illustrated by Michelle Walker

Interior & Cover layout by Vanessa Anderson
at NightOwlFreelance.com

Paperback ISBN-13: 978-1-949193-06-0
Hardcover ISBN-13: 978-1-949193-07-7

Printed in the U.S.A.

This story is dedicated to Lachlan,
you are an expression of our pure love.

Artwork dedicated to Cainan and Forrest,
my brave and curious explorers.

"BLESSED ARE THE CURIOUS
FOR THEY SHALL HAVE ADVENTURES."
— *ANON*

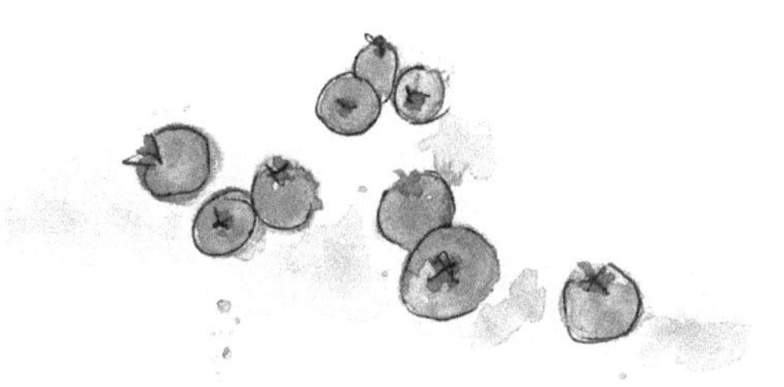

THE JOURNEY'S QUEST

IT ALL STARTED when we were getting packed for one of our many adventures. While my mum gathered the gear: all the food and stuff we might possibly need to make our camping trip a success, Daddy packed the car up just right so we all had room.

How to
Catch
a Bear
101
GUM

Daddy asked me, “What do you want to do when we get to the campsite?”

“Go on a hike,” I said.

Mumma suggested, “What about we go on a bear hunt, just like that book you love?”

“Yeah! Yeah!” I said super excited.

Then Daddy said, “Go get what you think we’ll need for our quest.”

As our journey began, I couldn't stop thinking of all the things we might find.

"Daddy, can we search for gold on our quest?" I said.

"Ooh, sure! We can lure the bear with gold," he said.

"Daddy, where will we put the bear when we find him? In the back seat?" I said.

FREE
GOLD

“Hmmm, I’m not sure a bear will fit in the back of the car. Maybe we should search for something smaller?” Daddy said.

“Like a mountain lion!” I suggested.

“Sure. Or a squirrel,” he said.

“Or a skunk,” I said.

“No, never a skunk!” he said.

That made me and Mumma laugh.

The whole car ride I saw many things
I never thought to search for, but they
weren't quite what I wanted to take home.

Most of the time I watched for animals in
the trees along the side of the road.

When camp was finally set up, it was like a new little home in the woods.

“Now can we go on our quest?” I said.

“Sure, have you thought of any other animals we might find?” asked Mumma.

“Yep! A porcupine!” I said.

“Think we could call him porky?” Daddy said smiling.

“That’s perfect!” I said.

Mumma and I laughed.

The woods had sounds I hadn't heard before. Some were scary until I learned what creature made the noise.

"Who whoo whooo cooksfroo. . . "

"What was that?" I said.

Mumma smiled. "That's a Barred Owl," she said. "It sounds like he's saying, who, who, who cooks for you?"

"You do," I said, snuggling into mumma.

"Whip-poor-will, whip-poor-will," I heard in the distance.

"And that was a Whippoorwill," Daddy assured me.

who

whoooo

whoo

whippoorwill

Then we heard a

thwack!

“Daddy, what animal says that?” I asked. “Uhh, well, I’m not sure that was an animal call, buddy,” he said.

“Yeah, that sounded like someone hitting a tree,” Mumma said.

She was calm, but I was a little scared. I scooched in between them as we talked about the sounds.

We heard crickets and peepers.

Daddy said a couple of the little squeaks could be chipmunks we were disturbing with the fire light.

As we were finishing up our bed time snack, Daddy made sure the fire was out.

Then we all shuffled into the tent.

I was looking forward to snuggling in our bed. It always felt so safe and warm between Mumma and Daddy.

I started to fall asleep, then all of a sudden...

AAAAAWOOOOOOOP!!!

Daddy whispered . . . "That might be an owl I've never heard."

I could tell Mumma was smiling when she said, "Or a squirrel."

"Maybe it was Bigfoot," I said.

"Maybe he's saying goodnight," Mumma encouraged.

"That Bigfoot is one smart fella," Daddy said.

"Daddy, can we go on a Bigfoot quest?"

"That's a quest for only the brave and fearless."

"I'm brave," I said.

Daddy hugged me tight. "You are so brave."

The next morning, after our breakfast of oatmeal, toast, and blueberries, we set out on our hike.

Daddy stood proud, stomped his walking stick on the ground, and said in a deep voice, “We shall now begin our official Bigfoot quest.”

Mumma giggled.

I was so excited, I danced, jumped, and ran in place.

We set off into the forest with the sun smiling down on us through the clouds.

We ventured through the woods, over giant rocks, and even some huge trees—so big they were like bridges.

“Why don’t my brave and fearless questors pick a spot for lunch,” Mumma said smiling.

We picked a really cool huge rock with a view of the mountainside.

While Mumma and Daddy laughed and talked a while, I decided to look around for any signs of Bigfoot.

Mumma and Daddy always let me explore on my own a bit when we go on hikes.

We hadn't seen anyone else all day because we had been walking the game trails.

Daddy says game trails are paths that animals make. Both Mumma and Daddy think those are more fun to follow. I agree.

I wandered off far enough where I couldn't see Mumma and Daddy, but I could still hear them laughing.

And then, right in front of me, I saw a big stack of sticks the size of small trees. They were all leaned against each other, like a teepee.

I yelled out, "MUMMA, DADDY—COME LOOK AT THIS!"

"Coming!" Mumma called out.

I could hear Daddy and Mumma coming toward me. They always know where I am.

I went into the teepee to look around. The ground was soft with pine needles and smelled like our puppy when she's wet from a bath.

"Wow!" Daddy said.

I peeked my head out. "Daddy you could fit in here." He's tall and big but very gentle.

Mumma poked her head in while Daddy walked around it. Mumma wrinkled her nose. "It stinks in here. Get out!" she said.

Daddy laughed. He knows Mumma hates bad smells.

"I think we could all fit in there together," Mumma said.

I smiled, because we always fit together.

"Do you think this is Bigfoot's home?" I asked.

"Sure could be," said Daddy.

"Come on, boys—we don't want to bother his home. That's not nice," Mumma said.

"Can we leave him a gift?" I asked.

Mumma smiled. "Sure." She gave me an apple from our lunch.

I placed it in the center of the teepee.

Daddy tousled my hair. “Great find,” he said.

I strutted down the trail with my parents.

THWACK!!!

Later that night, back at camp, we had full bellies and a cozy fire Daddy had built.

I fell asleep listening to Mumma and Daddy talk, laugh, and tell stories of their adventures.

I didn't even know they put me in bed until I woke to the loudest sound...

It startled me and Mumma awake. We stayed still and listened while Daddy snored.

"Daddy is calling the bears," Mumma joked.

That's when we heard it again, and I had to wake Daddy.

"Dadda! Dadda—Listen!"

We listened very hard.

“I think I hear the trees growing,” Daddy said with a smile.

That made Mumma laugh.

“I’m pretty sure that was Bigfoot,” I said, then I fell back to sleep.

I awoke in the morning before Mumma and Daddy, and I quietly snuck out of the tent into the morning light.

“Daddy!” I whispered really loud.

He scrambled out of the tent faster than our puppy eating dinner.

Mumma’s head was also poking out of the tent.

HOOOOOOOOO

Just outside the tent was the biggest footprint I had ever seen.

I was standing IN it!

Mumma and Daddy just stared at me and the numerous footprints in our campsite.

I smiled wide. “I guess Bigfoot wanted to play last night. Can we go find him to see if he can play now?”

Then a funny thing happened, my dad’s mouth moved, but I didn’t hear any words.

Mumma said quietly, “After breakfast.”

I knew to obey and couldn’t wait for Mumma and Daddy to start cooking. But breakfast took forever!

I just knew it was Bigfoot who left those prints.

I almost shouted with excitement when we started hiking. I knew where to go and took off with Mumma and Daddy in tow.

They kept telling me to slow down. But I couldn't wait!

We hiked a long time into the deep forest. I wasn't worried. I knew Daddy could find our way back.

All of a sudden, I heard rustling and small grunts. I knew it had to be Bigfoot! I pushed through a bunch of branches and to my surprise . . .

There was
the biggest porcupine
I'd ever seen!
It stared at me for a moment
and then scurried away.

We searched and searched but found no hint of our big curious neighbor.

“Daddy, we leave tomorrow, don’t we?” I said.

“Yeah, buddy, we do—you were really hoping to see Bigfoot, huh?” he said.

“Yeah, a little. Maybe next camping trip?”

Daddy tousled my hair, “You bet!” he said.

All the rest of our day I kept my eyes wide open and focused on any movement in the trees.

That night our fire was big. We roasted marshmallows and ate the rest of our snacks. We had a feast!

As the night quieted, my eyes grew heavy.

“Try not to be discouraged, honey,” Mumma said as she kissed and hugged me tight.

“Yeah, I’ve been searching for Bigfoot for years!” Daddy said with a little smile.

I fell asleep in the comfort of their hugs.

The morning seemed to go faster than any morning there. We checked one last time to make sure we got everything. “Leave no trace,” Mumma reminded us.

Daddy kneeled down and said, “Here, how about you pick a special spot to leave this.”

“Daddy, this is your lucky crystal,” I said.

“Yep. Now it’s yours to gift to Bigfoot. That way, next time we come, he’ll remember you.”

I was so happy.

While Daddy helped Mumma, I picked the *perfect* spot in the deep groove of a large log I had sat on during the whole trip.

“Feeling better?” Mumma asked.

“A little,” I said.

"All right, load up!" Daddy called out. "Goodbye, campsite," he said.

"See ya next time," sang Mumma.

As we pulled away, I stared out the back window . . .

ABOUT THE AUTHORS

ERNEST & CHRISTINE SOLAR are a team in all aspects of life. Together, they enjoy hiking, camping, reading, and hanging out with each other. They live in Lovettsville, Virginia with their son, Lachlan, his sisters, and an abundance of plants.

ABOUT THE ILLUSTRATOR

MICHELLE WALKER lives in Wilmington, North Carolina with her family. She enjoys spending time outdoors and finds nature to be her biggest inspiration for her artwork.

CPSIA information can be obtained
at www.ICGtesting.com
Printed in the USA
BVHW020150300921
617782BV00015B/786